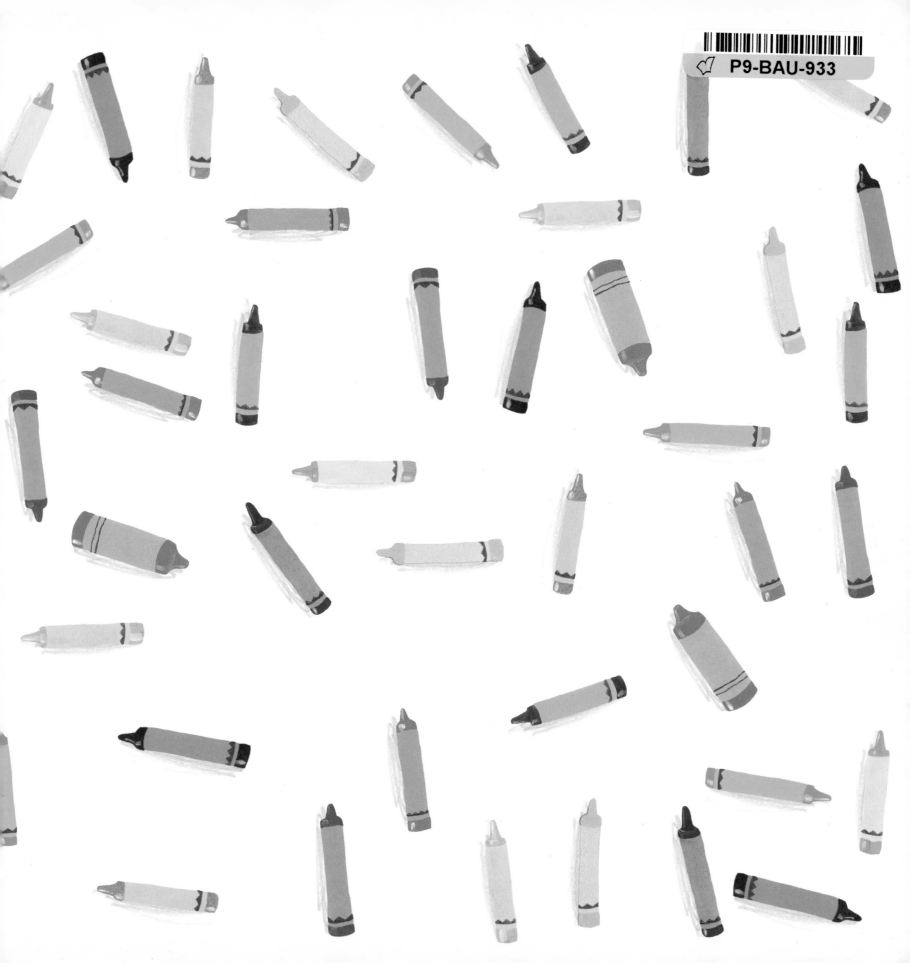

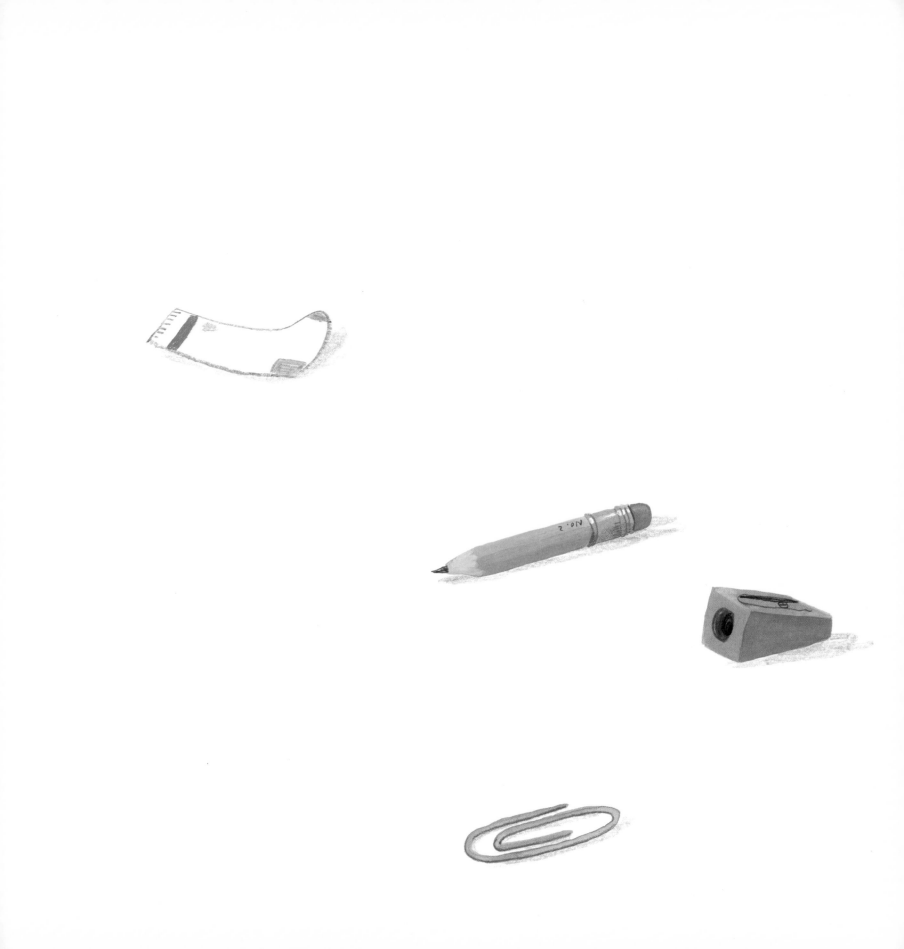

To my parents,
Charles and Charlene Daywalt,
who taught me to always make room for everyone.
—D.D.

For Logan.

—O.J.

The DAY the CRAYONS came HOME

DREW DAYWALT   OLIVER JEFFERS

PHILOMEL BOOKS   An Imprint of Penguin Group (USA)

One day, Duncan and his crayons were happily coloring together when a strange stack of postcards arrived for him in the mail . . .

Dear Duncan,

Not sure if you remember me. My name is MAROON CRAYON. You only colored with me once, to draw a scab, but whatever. Anyway, you LOST me TWO years ago in the couch, then your Dad SAT on me and BROKE ME IN HALF! I never would have SURVIVED had PAPERCLIP not NURSED me back to HEALTH. I'm finally better, so come get me! And can Paper Clip come too? He's really holding me together.

Sincerely,
Your marooned crayon,
MAROON CRAYON

Published by Coleman Ltd., Printed in the Republic of Ireland.

434

POSTAGE 20 15 THE COU...

BELFAST
4p

DUNCAN

Duncan's Bedroom

UPSTAIRS

THIS HOUSE

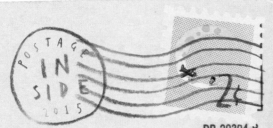

Dear Duncan,
No one likes peas.
No one even likes the color
 PEA GREEN.   So I'm changing
my name and RUNNing away
to see the WORLD.

 Sincerely,
 Esteban... the MAGNIFicent!
(the crayon formerly known as PEA GREEN)

post card

DUNCAN
DUNCAN's BEDroom
upstairs
This HOUSe

Sp MADE BY
SCAMPI PRESS, INC.
NEW YORK

Hi, DuNcan,

RITZ MOTEL
A lovely spot for year 'round recreation

It's me, NEON RED crayon.
REMEMBER that great vacation we
had with your Family? Remember
how we laughed when we drew a
PicTure of your Dad's SuNBurn?
Remember dropping me by the hotel
Pool when you left? clearly you
do <u>NOT</u>, BECAUSE I'M STILL HERE!
How could you miss me? Anyway.
After 8 months waiting for you to come
get me, I guess I'm walking BACK...

Your left behind Friend,
NEON Red CRAyon

POSTAGE LOST 2015

AIR TRAVEL 3¢ THREE

POST CARD

Duncan
Duncan's Room
DuNcan's House

PICKING COCONUTS
FUN IN THE SUN !

Duncan!
It's us... Yellow and ORANGE. We know we used to ARgue over which of us was the color of the SUN... But GUESS what? NEITHER of us wants to be the COLOR of the SUN anymore. Not since we were LEFT OUTSIDE and the SUN MELTED us... TOGETHER!! You know the REAL color of the SUN?? HOT. That's what. We're sorry for arguing. You can make GREEN the sun for all we care, just BRING US HOME!

Your not-so-sunny friends,
Yellow & ORANGE

AIR MAIL

SPACE USA 34¢

Post Card
Duncan
Duncan's room
INSIDE!
That House
there →

Hey Duncan,

I'm sure you don't recognize me...
after the horrors I've been through.
I think I was... TAN CRAYON?
or maybe... Burnt Sienna? I don't
know... I can't tell anymore. Have
you ever been eaten by a dog and puked
up on the living room rug? Because
I have... I HAVE BEEN EATEN BY A DOG
AND PUKED UP ON THE RUG, Duncan...
and it's NOT pretty. Not pretty at all...
I'm more carpet fuzz than crayon now.
Can you PLEASE bring me back?!

Your UNDIGESTIBLE friend,
Tan (or possibly Burnt Sienna?) Crayon

P4135

POSTAGE
2015
DOWNSTAIRS

FISH
8¢

Post Card

ADDRESS

Duncan

His Bedroom

Upstairs

Dearest Duncan,

um... Could you please
OPEN the FRONT DOOR?
I still need to see
the world...
Sincerely,
Esteban the
          Magnificent

Post Card

POSTAGE
20
15
THE DOOR

BROCCOLI

6p

Duncan

Duncan's Bedroom
Upstairs
This House

Rev. 1-4

Hey Duncan,
Remember last Halloween we told
your little brother there was a
GHOST under the BASEMENT stairs?
Then we drew that SCARY stuff on
the wall? Sure was funny when he ran
SCREAMING, right? But It wasn't so
funny when you FORGOT to take
me out of the BASEMENT! Please
come get me!
    I'm   kind   of... terribly...   horrified...

    Your   scared   friend,
    Glow   in   the   DARK   crayon

POST CARD

DUNCan
DUNCan's
Bedroom
UPStairs
THIS HOUSE

Dear DUNCAN,
Looks like I'm almost home!
Been through China, Canada, and
France... I think.
Just crossing New Jersey
by camel now!
New Jersey has GIANT
pyramids, right?

See ya soon,
Neon RED Crayon
P.S. Next stop, the NORTH pole
                    (I think)

POSTAGE
OUT
SIDE
2 0 1 5

22£

DUNCan
Duncan's Room
DUNCAN'S HOUSE

The Land of Gold

Duncan,
Does page 8 of "PIRATE Island" ring a bell?
Kind of a big payday for CAPtain GREENBeard
there, don't ya think? And NO BRONZE
or silver in that pile, huh? I told
you it'd make me blunt if you
colored each coin INDIVIDUALLy, But
would you listen? NOoo.
I Also told you those stupid crayon
sharpeners NEVER WORK. Did you
listen to that? Also NOOoo.
NOW I can't color ANYthing at ALL!

Your Pointless FRiend,
GOLD CRAYon

Duncan
DUNCAN'S ROOM
UPStairs

I HAD to
write it
for him.

This
IS NOT FUN
For ME either,
you KNow!

A Haul of Loot

A Bad Day for the Cabin Boy

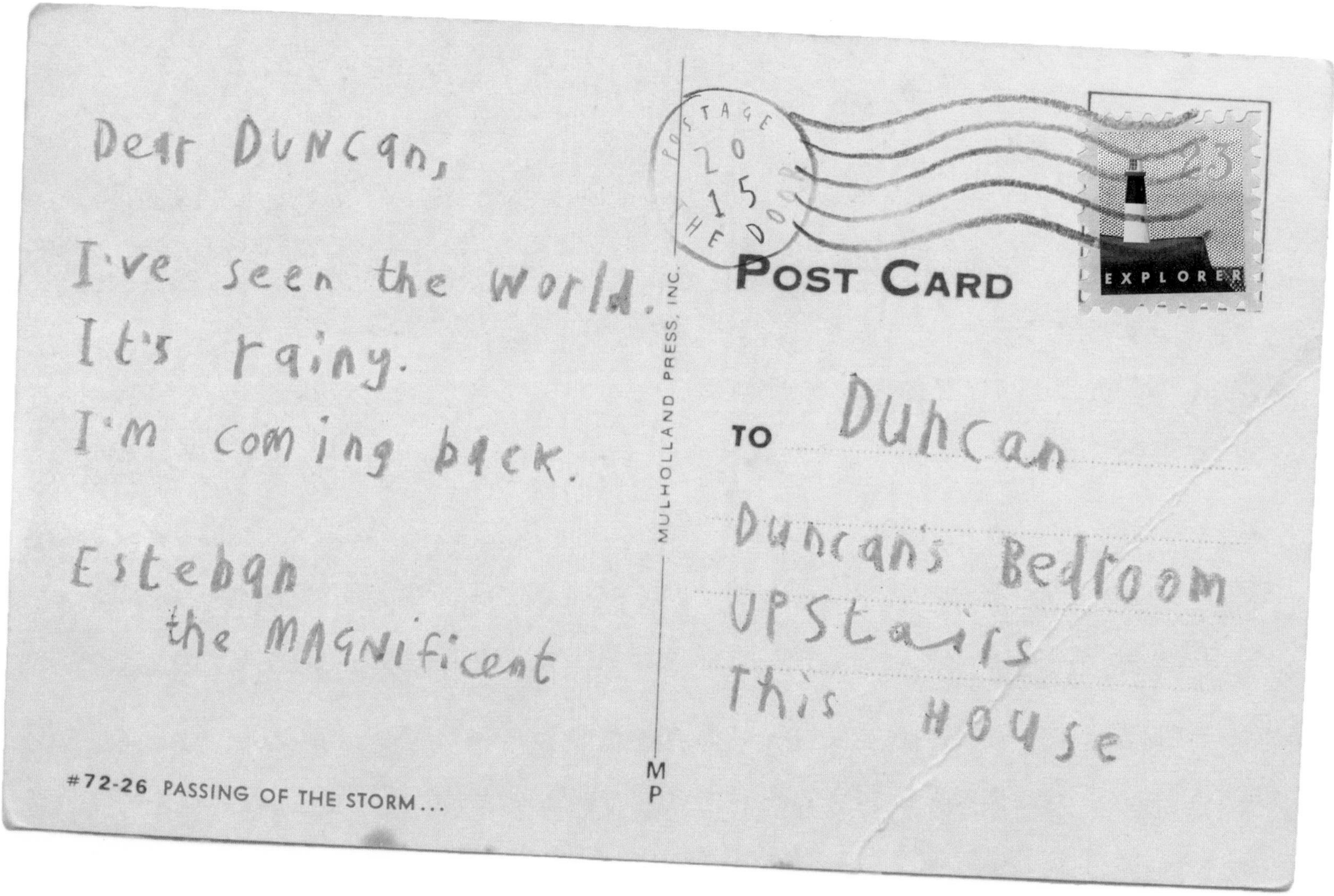

Dear DUNCan,

I've seen the world.
It's rainy.
I'm coming back.

Esteban
the MAGNificent

#72-26 PASSING OF THE STORM...

MULHOLLAND PRESS, INC.

M
P

POSTAGE
20
15
THE DOOR

EXPLORER 23

POST CARD

TO Duncan
Duncans Bedroom
UPStairs
This HOUSE

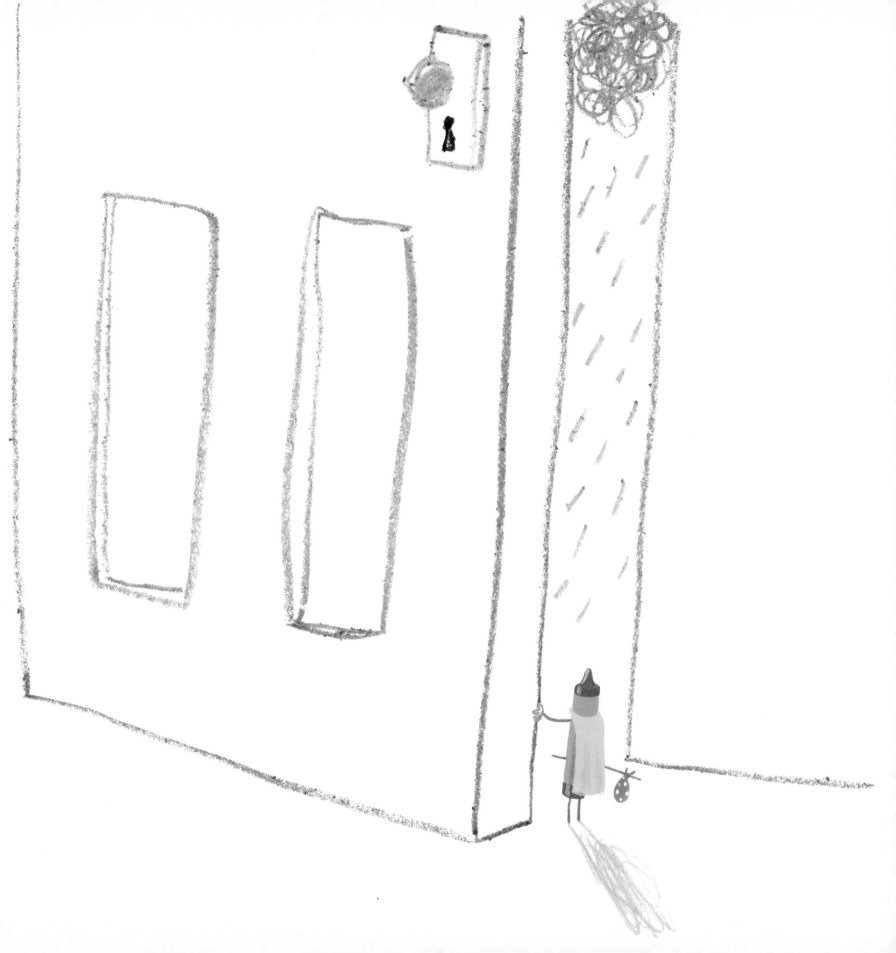

Hi, DuNCAN,

You're probably wondering why my head is stuck to Your SOCK? A question I ask myself every DAy. Well... it's because last week you left me in your pocket and I ended up in the DRYER. I landed on Your sock and now he's stuck to my head. Can you please come get me? Also, why does everything you wear still smell even after it's washed?

Your stinky-socky-stucky-
on-head buddy,
TURQUOISE Crayon
P.S. Sock says "Hi"

The awesome splendor of a thundering waterfall.

PHOTO BY: S. DACEY ® COLOR REPRODUCTION (REG. U. S. A. PAT. OFF.)

POSTAGE DOWN STAIRS 20 LOST

26 DUCKIE

POST CARD

DUNCAN
DunCan's
Room
upstairs

Dear Mr. Duncan,

I know I'm not your crayon. I know I belong to your Baby Brother, but I can't TAKE him anymore. In the last WEEK alone he's bitten the TOP of my HEAD, put me in the cat's NOSE, drawn on the WALL and tried to color GARBAGE with me! The WORST part is he is a TERRIBLE Artist! I can't tell what his drawings are. Donkeys? Monkeys? DONKEY-MONKEYS? Picasso said every child is an artist, but I dunno. I don't think he met your Brother. Please Rescue me.

Your desperate Friend,
BIG CHUNKY Toddler Crayon

l'art
orange
07¢
2015
INSIDE
POSTAGE

ADRESSE

M Duncan
Duncan's Room
Upstairs
This House

SKIING AND A FAST JUMP ALONG THE TRAIL

Duncan,
greetings from the
AMAZON Rain Forest.

Making GREAT TIME!
I think I'm almost home.

NEON RED crayon

Pub. by Maeve S. White Ridge Enterprise, 04102

POSTAGE OUTSIDE
2015

4¢
WINTER

DR-28060-B

post card

Duncan
DUNCAN'S Room
DUNCAN'S House

Hello, Duncan,

It's me, BROWN Crayon. You Know
EXACTly why I ran away, buddy!
Everyone thinks I get ALL the great coloring
jobs - candy Bars, puppies, ponies. Lucky me,
right? Bet they don't know what Else you
used me to color, do they? I didn't think so.
The rest of that drawing was great,
but did it really need that FINAL
BROWN scribble?
I'll come back, but please let's
stick to CANDY Bars, ok?

Your VERY embarrassed Friend,
BROWN CRAYON

IN THE MAINE WOODS

POST CARD

Duncan
DUNCAN'S ROOM
DUNCAN'S House
Next DOOR

INSIDE
2015
POSTAGE

VACATIONLAND
35¢
USA
Postage

Hey Duncan,

I'm sure you don't recognize me... after the horrors I've been through. I think I was... Tan CRAYON? or maybe... Burnt Sienna? I don't know... I can't tell anymore. Have you ever been eaten by a dog and puked up on the living room rug? Because I have... I HAVE BEEN EATEN BY A DOG AND HAVE PUKED UP ON THE RUG, Duncan... and it's NOT pretty. Not pretty at all... I'm more carpet fuzz than crayon now. Can you PLEASE bring me back?!

Your UNDIGESTIBLE friend,
Tan (or possibly Burnt Sienna?) Crayon

P4135

POSTAGE 2015 DOWNST...

FISH

8¢

Post Card
ADDRESS

Duncan
His Bed...
UPSTA...

Dear Duncan,

Not sure if you remember me. My... MAROON CRAYON. You only... once, to draw a scab, but wh... you LOST me TWO year... couch, then your Dad SAT... BROKE ME IN HAL... ever would have SURVIVED h... ...PER clip not NURSED me... alth. I'm Finall... get me!

P.S. Next stop the North Pole. ...oom, RED Crayon (I think)

GIZA - The Pyramids
الجيزة - الأهرامات

MULHOLLAND PRESS, INC.

...NG OF THE STORM...

...MAGNIFICENT

...ing back.

...the world

...can!

Post Card

POSTAGE 2015 THE DOO...

TO
Dunca...
Duncan's Be...
UPStairs...
This Hous...

UPStairs This House
Duncan's Room
M Duncan

ADRESSE

POSTAGE 2015 INSIR...

...Artist ...s are... ...ers. ...WORST ...NOSE, ...op of ...the ...but ...crayon. I know ...m you wil... ...

How...
After 8 m...
get me, I guess...

Your left o...
NEON Red ...

Dear Mr. Duncan, CARTE POSTALE

THE MOTEL
N
Playground 273 M
Tobaccan 106 M
Swimming Pool ... M
North Pole
Air-Conditioning 373 M
Free Radios 70 M
Saturn 746 M
Duncan's Room 338 M

SU...
...INT...
...t?

D...
DUnc...
DUNCA...

Duncan was sad to learn of all the crayons he'd lost, forgotten, broken or neglected over the years. So he ran around gathering them up.

But Duncan's crayons were all so damaged and differently shaped than they used to be that they no longer fit in the crayon box.

So Duncan had an idea . . .

He built a place where each crayon would *always* feel at home.

There's NO DOGS down there, are there?

Nope! No Turkeys either!

CRAYONS

oh you Flatter me, but it's not REAL Chocolate

Let's HAVE a PARTY!

This one is from my BLUE Period

But it's not really Blue... more lilac!

ALSO BY DREW DAYWALT AND OLIVER JEFFERS:

The Day the Crayons Quit

PHILOMEL BOOKS
Published by the Penguin Group | Penguin Group (USA) LLC
375 Hudson Street, New York, NY 10014

USA | Canada | UK | Ireland | Australia | New Zealand | India | South Africa | China
penguin.com | A Penguin Random House Company

Library of Congress Cataloging-in-Publication Data
Daywalt, Drew, author.
The day the crayons came home / by Drew Daywalt ; pictures by Oliver Jeffers.
pages cm   Companion book to: The day the crayons quit.   Summary: One day, Duncan is happily coloring with his crayons
when a stack of postcards arrives in the mail from his former crayons, each of which has run away or been left behind,
and all of which want to come home.   [1. Crayons—Fiction. 2. Postcards—Fiction. 3. Color—Fiction.] I. Jeffers, Oliver,
illustrator. II. Title. PZ7.D3388Dat 2015 [E]—dc23 2015003512

Manufactured in China by RR Donnelley Asia Printing Solutions Ltd.
ISBN 978-0-399-17275-5
1 3 5 7 9 10 8 6 4 2

Edited by Michael Green.   Text set in 20-point Mercury Text G1.
The art for this book was made with crayons, the Postal Service, and a cardboard box.

GREETINGS FROM **NEITHER HERE NOR T...**

POST·CARD

THE CRAYON CASTLE

1 Mile west of Duncan's Bedroom. Left out of the Garage.

CRAYON INN MOTEL

Need to Get Out of the Box? Enjoy Our Air Conditioned Suites!

RESTAURANT LOUNGE

AP 10 *CRAYON POSTCARD. MADE BY ME*

Wish you were here